This book belongs to:

Retold by Gaby Goldsack
Illustrated by Emma Lake

Language consultant: Betty Root

This edition published by Parragon in 2013
Parragon
Chartist House
15–17 Trim Street
Bath BA1 1HA, UK
www.parragon.com

ISBN 978-1-4454-7068-9

Printed in China

Little Red Riding Hood

Bath · New York · Singapore · Hong Kong · Cologne · Delhi
Melbourne · Amsterdam · Johannesburg · Shenzhen

Helping Your Child to Read

Learning to read is an exciting challenge for most children. From a very early age, sharing story books with children, talking about the pictures and guessing what might happen next are all very important parts of the reading experience.

Sharing reading

Set aside a regular quiet time to share reading with younger children, or to be on hand to encourage older children as they develop into independent readers.

This book is intended to encourage and support the early stages of learning to read. It is a well-loved tale that children will happily listen to again and again. Familiarity helps children to identify some of the words and phrases.

When you feel your child is ready to move on a little, encourage him or her to join in so that you read the story aloud together. Always pause to talk about the pictures. The easy-to-read speech bubbles in this book provide an excellent 'joining-in' activity. The bright, clear illustrations and matching text will help children to understand the story.

Building confidence

In time, children will want to read *to* you. When this happens, be patient and give continual praise. They may not read all the words correctly, but children's substitutions are often very good guesses.

The repetition in each book is particularly helpful for building confidence. If your child cannot read a particular word, go back to the beginning of the sentence and read it together so the meaning is not lost. Most importantly, do not continue if your child is tired or simply in need of a change.

Reading alone

The next step is to ask your child to read alone. Try to be on hand to give help and support. Remember to give lots of encouragement and praise. This will ensure that children will find reading an enjoyable and rewarding experience.

Once upon a time there was a little girl. She wore a red hood and cloak. Everyone called her Little Red Riding Hood.

One day, Little Red Riding Hood's mother said,

"Granny is ill. Take her this basket of food."

Little Red Riding Hood's granny
lived on the other side
of the wood.

Little Red Riding Hood walked through the wood towards her granny's house.

She did not see a hungry wolf watching her.

The hungry wolf jumped out in front of
Little Red Riding Hood.

"Where are you going?" he asked.

"I'm taking this basket of food to Granny, who is ill," said Little Red Riding Hood.

To Granny's house.

13

"Where does your granny live?" asked the wolf.

"She lives in a house on the other side of the wood." said Little Red Riding Hood.

The hungry wolf smiled.

Why don't you pick some flowers?

"Why don't you pick flowers for your granny?" he said.

"What a good idea," said Little Red Riding Hood.

Little Red Riding Hood put down her basket to pick some flowers.

The hungry wolf smiled.

Then he ran off to Granny's house.

When he got there, the hungry wolf ate Granny in one big gulp.

But he was still hungry!

The hungry wolf put on Granny's cap
and glasses. Then he got into Granny's
bed and waited for Little Red
Riding Hood.

He did not have to wait long.
Little Red Riding Hood walked in.

"Hello, Granny," said Little Red Riding
Hood. Then she stopped and looked.

"Granny, what big eyes you have!"
said Little Red Riding Hood.

"All the better to see you with," said the hungry wolf.

"Granny, what big ears you have!" said Little Red Riding Hood.

"All the better to hear you with," said the hungry wolf.

"Granny, what big teeth you have!" said Little Red Riding Hood.

"All the better to eat you with," said the hungry wolf.

Little Red Riding Hood screamed.

Suddenly, the hungry wolf jumped out
of bed and...

...ate Little Red Riding Hood in one big gulp!

Now the wolf was not hungry any more. He was very full. He lay on Granny's bed and fell asleep.

ZZZZZZZZZZZZZZZZZ

In the wood, a woodcutter heard Little Red Riding Hood scream.

He ran into the house. He saw the wolf asleep on Granny's bed and...

...killed it with his axe!

"Let us out!" cried Little Red Riding Hood and Granny from inside the wolf's tummy.

The woodcutter cut open the wolf's tummy. Out jumped Little Red Riding Hood and Granny.

Granny was so pleased to be saved that she invited the woodcutter to tea!

Read and Say

How many of these words can you say?
The pictures will help you. Look back in
your book and see if you can find the
words in the story.

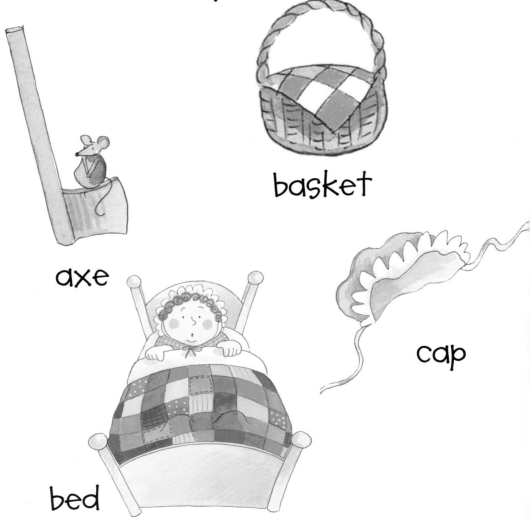

basket

axe

cap

bed

ears

flowers

eyes

glasses

Granny

food

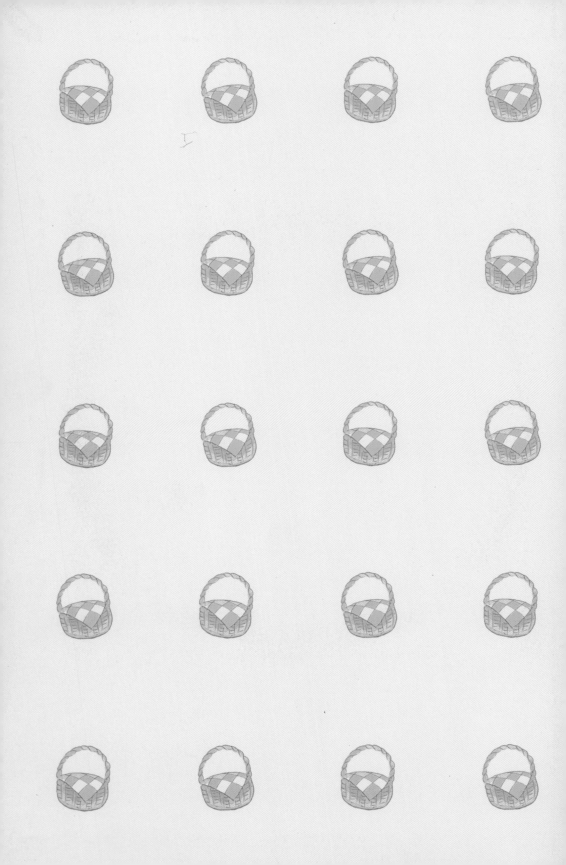